BROBOT
BEDTIME

A story by **SUDIPTA BARDHAN-QUALLEN**
Pictures by **SCOTT CAMPBELL**

Abrams Books for Young Readers
New York

THE ILLUSTRATIONS IN THIS BOOK WERE MADE WITH WATERCOLOR AND PENCIL.

Cataloging-in-Publication Data has been applied for and may be obtained from the Library of Congress.

ISBN: 978-1-4197-2290-5

Printed and bound in China
10 9 8 7 6 5 4 3 2 1

Abrams Books for Young Readers are available at special discounts when purchased in quantity for
premiums and promotions as well as fundraising or educational use. Special editions can also be
created to specification. For details, contact specialsales@abramsbooks.com or the address below.

ABRAMS The Art of Books
115 West 18th Street, New York, NY 10011
abramsbooks.com

Maybe if you drink a nice cup of oil,
the flick-ups will go away.